A Parents Magazine
READ ALOUD AND EASY READING PROGRAM® Original.

# A GARDEN
# FOR
# MISS MOUSE

To R.H.S. for his
P.A.T.I.E.N.C.E.——*M.M.*


To Louise——*C.S.*

Library of Congress Cataloging in Publication Data
Muntean, Michaela. A garden for Miss Mouse.
SUMMARY: Miss Mouse plants a garden which soon
becomes more than she can handle.
[1. Gardening — Fiction.  2. Stories in rhyme.]
I. Santoro, Christopher, ill.  II. Title.
PZ8.3.M89Gar  [E]  82-2135
ISBN 0-8193-1083-2  AACR2
ISBN 0-8193-1084-0  (lib. bdg.)

# A GARDEN
# FOR
# MISS MOUSE

by

## Michaela Muntean

pictures by

## Christopher Santoro

Parents Magazine Press
New York

Every first of April
Miss Mouse tills and rakes and hoes.
Then she plants a garden
in neat and tidy rows.

A little row of carrots,
a little row of beans,
and then another little row
of lovely lettuce greens.

But this year when she started
to plant her little rows,
she stopped and said quite suddenly,
"This bores me to my toes!"

"I know what I will do!" she cried,
and then she danced a jig.
She grabbed her biggest shovel,
and she began to dig.

"I'll plant the biggest garden
ever seen by any mouse!"
Then up came every bit of land
all around her house.

Next she had to plant the seeds.
It took her all day long.
But all the while she planted,
she sang a planting song:

Plant a little of this,
and a little of that.
Cover the seed,
and give it a pat!

Every day she hoed and raked.
She tilled and pulled the weeds.

And soon green plants were springing up where she had planted seeds.

The plants all started growing.
They grew and grew and grew.
And everyone in Mouseville
came to *aah* and *ooh*.

"Oh, what lovely peas!" they cried.
"And see that beanstalk climb!"
Reporters took Miss Mouse's picture
for the *Mouseville Times*.

EXTRA

The Mouseville Times

5¢

# SEE HER GARDEN GROW!!

DATELINE MOUSEVILLE,
THE GARDEN OF MISS
MOUSE HAS GROWN
ENORMOUS! WHEN
ASKED WHY SHE DID IT,
MISS MOUSE CONFESSED,
"THE SMALLER GARDEN
SIMPLY BORED ME."

MISS MOUSE HAS GROWN
LETTUCE, CARROTS,
CELERY, AND BROCCOLI,
TO NAME JUST A FEW
OF HER VEGETABLES.

FOR A COMPLETE LISTING,
TURN TO TODAY'S
GARDENING SECTION.

NEIGHBORS REPORT THAT
THEY ARE QUICKLY LOSING
SIGHT OF THE HOUSE.
THEY ARE STANDING BY
IN CASE MISS MOUSE
NEEDS THEIR HELP.

PHOTO: J. P. SQUEEK

SEE OUR EXCLUSIVE STORY ON MISS MOUSE INSIDE...

The garden grew much bigger,
and then it grew some more.
It covered all the windows,
it covered the front door!

That garden was enormous,
and the plants so very high,
that Miss Mouse used a flagpole
to get her laundry dry.

The mailman left her letters
atop a beanstalk vine,
while Miss Mouse proudly laughed and said
"Isn't my garden fine!"

Then one day she woke to find
five mushrooms on her sheet,
ten pea pods on her pillow,
six peppers at her feet!

There were green beans in the basement,
and wax beans on the wall.

There was celery on the ceiling.
There were pumpkins in the hall!

Tomatoes in the bathtub!
Spinach on a chair!
Turnips on the table,
and zucchini *everywhere!*

Cabbage in the kitchen,
corn cobs in the hutch.
"Oh, my goodness!" cried Miss Mouse.
"My garden's grown too much!"

She knew she had to call for help,
but couldn't find the phone.
Then finally she found it
where some brussel sprouts had grown.

She called her best friend Field Mouse.
She asked him to come quick.
"Bring everyone you know!" she cried.
"There are vegetables to pick!"

So everyone in Mouseville
rushed out to help Miss Mouse.
"Where are you?" they cried helplessly.
"We cannot see your house!"

"My garden's growing everywhere!"
her friends could hear her shout.
"Please start picking vegetables
for I cannot get out!"

And so they started picking
fruit and vegetables galore.
They picked more kinds of vegetables
than you've seen in any store.

When finally they found Miss Mouse,
she cried, "How could I know
that this is what would happen
when things began to grow!"

"Don't worry," Field Mouse told her.
"It isn't all that bad.
We'll make the biggest salad
that we have ever had!"

All day they made that salad.
They chopped and tossed and peeled.

Then they had a garden party on Mouseville's football field.

"Good-bye and thank you," said Miss Mouse
when all her friends were going.
"Next year I'll keep my garden small.
It won't do too much growing!"

## About the Author

MICHAELA MUNTEAN tried organic gardening one summer and, to her surprise, the tomato plants grew seven feet high. That's when A GARDEN FOR MISS MOUSE was born.

Ms. Muntean was a children's book and magazine editor before she turned to writing full time. She has written many well-loved children's books, including THE VERY BUMPY BUS RIDE for Parents.

Ms. Muntean lives in New York City.

## About the Artist

CHRISTOPHER SANTORO has a garden on the terrace of his apartment. But it's the apartment itself that reminds him of Miss Mouse's garden. "It's always overgrown with materials I use as models for the pictures I'm working on," he explains.

Mr. Santoro has illustrated many children's books, including another story written by Michaela Muntean. This is his first book for Parents.

Mr. Santoro lives in New York City.

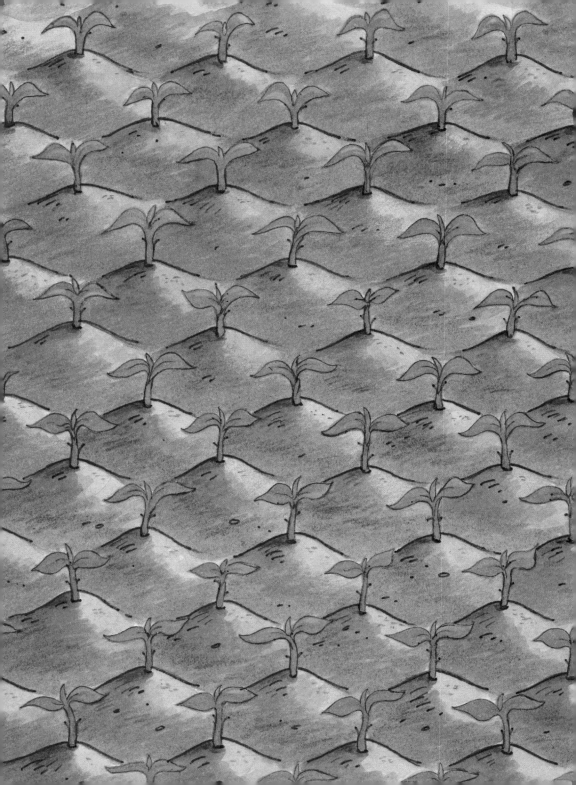